FIVE BUSY BEAVERS

Stella Partheniou
Grasso

illustrated by
Christine Battuz

Sky Pony Press
New York

Sky Pony Press books may be purchased in bulk at special discounts for sales promotion, corporate gifts, fund-raising, or educational purposes. Special editions can also be created to specifications. For details, contact the Special Sales Department, Skyhorse Publishing, 307 West 36th Street, 11th Floor, New York, NY 10018 or info@skyhorsepublishing.com.

Sky Pony® is a registered trademark of Skyhorse Publishing, Inc.®, a Delaware corporation.

www.skyponypress.com

www.stellapartheniougrasso.com

10 9 8 7 6 5 4 3 2 1

Manufactured in China, November 2017
This product conforms to CPSIA 2008

Library of Congress Cataloging-in-Publication Data is available on file.

Cover design by Kate Gartner
Cover illustration by Christine Battuz

Print ISBN: 978-1-5107-2145-6
E-book ISBN: 978-1-5107-2146-3

To Mom and Dad, who were never too busy
to read to me. Thank you for everything.
— S.P.G.

To my friend/sister, Anne-Marie.
— C.B.

Five busy beavers building up a dam,
closing off the river where the salmon swam.
Gnawing down trees,
and ferrying the logs.
Slapping on the mud
that they gathered from the bog.

Along came a muskrat,
who wanted to play.
And one little beaver swam away.

Four busy beavers chewing on some wood,

chopping down trees as fast as they could.

Poplars and willows,

maple trees and beech.

Searching through the forest,

they found a bit of each.

Along came a heron,
who wanted to play.
And one little beaver scampered away.

Three busy beavers dragging back the logs,
digging up canals that ran into the bog.
Pushing to the river,
and swimming to the lake.
Paddling their feet,
with no time to take a break.

Along came some chorus frogs,
who wanted to play.
And one little beaver frolicked away.

Two busy beavers gathering mud and silt,
diving to the riverbed until the dam was built.
Patching up the holes,
and filling in the cracks.
Thumping their tails
in a rhythm of smacks.

Along came a turtle,

who wanted to play.

And one little beaver waddled away.

One busy beaver in the setting sun,
working very hard until the job was done.
Checking for leaks,
and tidying the sticks.
Shoring up the dam,
using all a beaver's tricks.

Along came a firefly,
to light up the way.
And one tired beaver paddled away.

Four busy beavers and their playful friends,
gathered at the lodge with a plan to make amends.
Stringing up flowers,
making water lily pie.
Humming while they worked,
to make the time go by.

Along came a beaver with weary eyes . . .

. . . who was greeted at the door with a big

"Surprise!"

Life in a Beaver Pond

Beavers use rocks, branches, and mud to build dams that block rivers and create wetlands. Here, beaver parents teach their kits how to build cozy lodges and waterproof dams. The whole colony works together to keep the dam strong. The world's biggest beaver dam is in Wood Buffalo National Park in Alberta, Canada. It probably took about twenty-five years and the work of eight generations of beavers to get as big as it is!

Sometimes a **muskrat** will sneak into a beaver lodge for a nap while the beavers are out. When the beavers come back to sleep, the muskrat darts away. Muskrats use cattails and grasses to make their own lodges, called push-ups. Push-ups aren't as big or sturdy as beaver lodges, but they are cozy.

The biggest **heron** in North America is the great blue heron. Herons like to live in large colonies. A single tree will hold many nests, sort of like an apartment building. Beaver ponds are the perfect nesting ground for these birds. The shallow waters attract fish, bugs, and small animals. When herons spot a tasty snack, they use their long beaks to quickly snatch it up.

Male **chorus frogs** chirp loudly to attract females to shallow water. The canals beavers dig to transport logs back to their ponds are deep enough for the frogs to lay their eggs in, but too shallow for any big fish that might want to eat them. To avoid predators, some chorus frogs can throw their voices to sound like they're calling from a different part of the pond.

The **Blanding's turtle** is an endangered species in the United States. Its upturned mouth looks like it's always smiling. These turtles are shy, though. They like beaver ponds because they can dive in and hide in the mud for hours. They can also use their special hinged shells for hiding. The turtle can tuck in its head and feet and shut its shell up tightly until it's ready to come out.

Fireflies can be found across the eastern United States, including near beaver ponds, where the soil is moist and there's lots of tall grass to nest in. Fireflies are actually beetles. Their delicate wings tuck under a hard shell when they're resting. There are over two thousand different kinds of fireflies. Not all of them produce light. Those that do use their flashes to communicate with one another.